Tilly and the Blue Pearl

Tilly and the Blue Pearl

Angela McAllister
Illustrated by Maxine Lee

Orion
Children's Books

First published in Great Britain in 2015 by Orion Children's Books
an imprint of Hachette Children's Group
and published by Hodder and Stoughton Limited
Orion House
5 Upper Saint Martin's Lane
London WC2H 9EA
An Hachette UK Company

1 3 5 7 9 10 8 6 4 2

Text © Angela McAllister 2015
Illustrations © Maxine Lee 2015

The paper and board used in this paperback are natural and
recyclable products made from wood grown in sustainable forests.
The manufacturing processes conform to the environmental
regulations of the country of origin.

A catalogue record for this book
is available from the British Library.

ISBN 978 1 4440 1362 7

For Kimberley

Contents

Chapter One

Tilly was a mermaid. She lived in the warm, sunny water of Crystal Bay.

One morning, she sat outside
her coral cave, thinking hard.

Her pet seahorse, Sparkle,
swam up and tickled her tail.

"I'm sorry, Sparkle," said Tilly,
"I can't play now. I'm trying to think
of a present for my friend, Marina.
It's her birthday tomorrow."

Sparkle found a spotty shell.
"That's pretty," said Tilly, "but
Marina has lots of shells. I want to
give her something special."

At that moment, Turtle paddled by.
"Hello, Tilly," he called. "Can't
stop!"

Turtle was followed by a school
of angel fish.
　　Then three dolphins rushed past.
　　After them came a noisy family
of crabs.

"Where is everyone going?"
said Tilly. "Something must be
happening. Come on, Sparkle.
Let's find out."

Chapter Two

Tilly and Sparkle followed everyone
to Craggy Rock, where a big crowd
had gathered.

"What's happening?" Tilly
asked a lobster.

"We're waiting to see the
Mermaid Queen pass by," said
the lobster. "She is taking her
princesses to visit King Neptune."

Tilly was very excited.

"I've never seen the Mermaid
Queen," she told Sparkle.

Tilly found a good place to watch and waited. Suddenly, she felt somebody at her side. It was Marina.

"Isn't this fun?" said Marina. "I wonder what the Queen will be wearing. Look, they're coming!"

"Make way for Her Majesty!" cried a pair of swordfish.

Behind them was an octopus playing a trumpet shell, which made the jellyfish giggle.

At last, the Mermaid Queen appeared, with her four little princesses.

The Mermaid Queen wore a silver crown in her golden hair and a green, shimmery cloak.

"Isn't she *wonderful*?" said Marina.

The four princesses looked very happy.

"I wish I could be their sister for a day," sighed Tilly.

The youngest princess slowed down to wave to the crowd.

"Oh dear," said Tilly, "she'll get left behind."

But the Queen stopped and waited.

Marina gazed at the Queen. "What beautiful blue pearls," she said. "I *wish* I had a necklace like that!"

Tilly smiled. "I've got the perfect idea for Marina's present," she whispered to Sparkle. "I'll make her a necklace!"

Chapter Three

"What shall we do now?" said Tilly.

"Let's play in the shipwreck," said Marina. "It's my favourite place to explore."

The way to the shipwreck was past spooky Seaweed Forest.

The forest was thick with seaweed that grew so high you couldn't see the top.

Tilly, Marina and Sparkle stayed close together. "I don't like this place," said Tilly. "It's full of scary shadows."

"Even the water is cold here," Marina said.

But soon they came to a bright, sandy clearing, and there was the shipwreck.

Tilly, Marina and Sparkle had
fun all afternoon, swimming in and
out of the cabins and portholes.

Tilly looked out for something
pretty to make a necklace for Marina,
but she didn't see anything special.

On their way back past the forest,
Tilly spotted something gleaming
among the roots of the giant seaweed.

It was a **blue pearl!**
That's perfect, she thought.

When they were almost home,
Tilly stopped. "Oh dear, I've lost a
hair comb," she said. "It must have
fallen out at the shipwreck."

"I'll go back with you," said
Marina.

"No, don't worry," said Tilly.
Marina gave her friend a hug.
"Good luck, then," she said.
"I hope you find it, Tilly. See
you tomorrow."

Chapter Four

"I haven't really lost my hair comb," Tilly told Sparkle. "I'm going back to the Seaweed Forest to get a blue pearl for Marina's necklace."

When Sparkle heard that, he turned and swam home again.

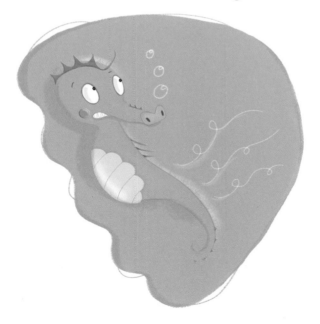

The Seaweed Forest felt even
more spooky, now Tilly was alone.

Tilly found the place she'd seen
the pearl and started to hunt for it.

She looked under every stone
and shell, but it wasn't there.

"How can it have disappeared?"
she wondered.

Suddenly Tilly heard a cry.
"Help!" a voice called.

It was coming from inside
the forest!

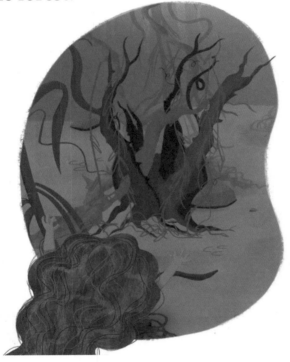

Tilly swam closer. The giant
seaweed swirled above her head.
The chilly water made her shiver.

"Help!" the voice cried again.

Tilly knew she had to be brave. With a flick of her tail she swam inside and pushed her way towards the voice.

As she went deeper into the forest, her long hair became tangled in the seaweed. She tried to tug herself free, but she was trapped!

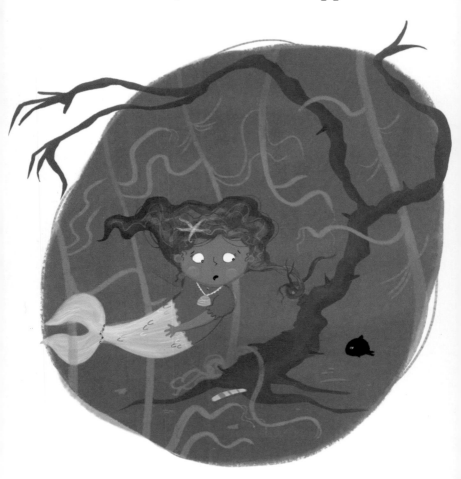

Tilly noticed a shell lying nearby. She stretched out her hand and just managed to reach it. Quick as a flash, she cut herself free and swam on.

"Help!" cried the voice again.

"I'm coming!" said Tilly.

Chapter Five

To Tilly's surprise, when she parted the seaweed, there was the youngest princess, tied up in a terrible knot!

The princess was very pleased to see Tilly. "I thought nobody would hear me!" she said.

"What's your name?" asked Tilly.

"I'm Cleo," said the princess. "I was looking for something and I got all tangled up."

Tilly cut away the seaweed. "I saw you going to visit King Neptune this morning," she said.

"It was fun," said Cleo, "but now I want to go home."

When Cleo was free, she thanked Tilly and picked up her little golden purse that was lying on the sand.

"I'll take you home," said Tilly.
The girls tied up their hair so
they wouldn't get caught again,
and slowly made their way out of
the forest.

"What a horrible place," said
Tilly, when they finally came out
into bright water. "I've always been
afraid of it."

"You still came to save me,
though," said Cleo. "That was
very brave."

Tilly told Cleo about the blue pearl she had been looking for to make Marina a necklace.

"Oh dear," said Cleo. She hugged her purse tight.

Soon they came to a shining white palace.

"Oh, it's beautiful!" said Tilly.

As Tilly followed Cleo, she remembered her wish to be a princess that morning. So this is what it feels like, she thought.

They found the Mermaid Queen
in the palace garden.

"Where have you been, Cleo?"
she said. "I've been so worried."

"I got caught in the Seaweed
Forest," said Cleo. "Tilly rescued
me."

And to Tilly's amazement, she opened her purse and tipped out...

a dozen blue pearls!

"My necklace," gasped the Queen. "I broke it on the way home from our visit to King Neptune," she explained to Tilly. "But you mustn't go into the forest alone, Cleo. Even if it *is* for a kind reason."

Tilly tried to hide her disappointment. She had wanted to give Marina a wonderful surprise. Now she knew for sure that she'd have nothing to give her at all.

Cleo saw her sad face.

"Tilly was looking for a pearl to make a necklace for her friend," she told the Queen.

The Mermaid Queen smiled. "Well, I have plenty, Tilly," she said. "Here is a pearl to thank you for helping Cleo," she said, "and another for your friend."

"Oh, **thank you**, your Majesty!"
said Tilly.

Chapter Six

When Tilly got home, she set to work
to make something very special.

Next day, Marina opened her present excitedly. "It's *wonderful*, thank you, Tilly," she said. "I feel like a princess! Where did you find such a beautiful blue pearl?"

Tilly told Marina all about Cleo and the Mermaid Queen.

"That's amazing!" said Marina. "Is this really from the Queen's own necklace?"

"Yes," said Tilly. "It's really true!"

At that moment, Cleo appeared. "Can I come to play?" she asked.

"Of course!" said Tilly.

"Happy Birthday, Marina," said Cleo. "I've brought you a present." And she gave Marina a gold purse for her necklace.

"These are the best birthday presents ever," said Marina happily.

Tilly smiled. "Your birthday brought me an adventure and a new friend too," she said. "So, where shall we play?"

The three friends looked at each other.

"Not the Seaweed Forest!" they all said, laughing.

What are you going to read next?

Have more adventures with
Horrid Henry,

or save the day with Anthony Ant!

Become a
superhero with Monstar,

float off to
sea with
Algy,

or have your very own Pirates' Picnic.

Grow carrots with

Lottie and Dottie,

make magic with The Witch Dog,

and cast a spell with

The Three Little Magicians.

Enjoy all the Early Readers.